This book belongs to:

_____

Disney
Tuck-in Tales

Adventure Stories

Tuck-in Tales

Adventure
Stories

SCHOLASTIC INC.

New York   Toronto   London   Auckland   Sydney
Mexico City   New Delhi   Hong Kong   Buenos Aires

Published by Scholastic Inc.,
90 Old Sherman Turnpike, Danbury, Connecticut 06816.

ISBN 0-439-89488-3

Printed in the U.S.A.
First printing, October 2006

Story illustrations by Alvin S. White Studio
Designed by North Woods Design Group

CONTENTS

The Blue Box
Mystery

Winnie the Pooh was strolling through the Hundred-Acre Wood one day when he stumbled upon a strange object.

"Oh, my," said Pooh. "It's a box! I wonder if it's someone's birthday—although it doesn't look like a birthday-present type of box. Perhaps Piglet will know whose it is."

By the time he reached Piglet's house, Pooh noticed he had a grumbling, fluttery feeling in his tummy that made him think of honey. So naturally when Piglet invited him in for a bite to eat, Pooh said yes and he sat down for a little honey and some milk. And then he had a little more honey and a little more milk. Until finally, Pooh was feeling full and happy.

"Well, it was nice of you to have me in, Piglet," said Pooh. "I suppose I should be going now."

"Don't forget your blue box," said Piglet.

"My what?" wondered Pooh.

"Your blue box," Piglet said. "You brought it with you when you came."

"Isn't it *your* blue box?" asked Pooh.

"No," said Piglet. "I don't think I own any blue boxes."

"Then whose is it?" Pooh asked.

"I thought it was yours because you brought it with you," said Piglet.

"Yes," said Pooh. "But I only brought it with me because I didn't know whose it was. I just knew that it was a box. But now that you mention it, it is blue, too, isn't it?"

"Oh, m-m-my!" cried Piglet suddenly. "You don't suppose it belongs to a h-h-heffalump, do you?"

"Well, I don't think so," Pooh said. "But I don't think not, either."

"Oh, Pooh!" squealed Piglet. "What if he followed you here? M-m-maybe there's a heffalump outside my door right now, waiting to gobble us up! We must hide!"

So Pooh and Piglet hid under Piglet's bed. After a while, there was a loud knocking at the door.

"H-h-he's here!" Piglet cried.

Again there was a loud knocking!

"Piglet?" said Pooh. "I've just had a thought. Don't heffalumps and other monsters like to hide under beds?"

"I think so," shivered Piglet.

"So, if this heffalump breaks through your door, do you think the first place he might go is—"

"Right where we are!" Piglet squealed, as he raced out from under the bed. Piglet headed straight for the closet, while Pooh—who had become wedged under the bed—struggled to get free.

"Oh, Pooh, hurry!" cried Piglet. Just then the door flew open and in bounced—Tigger!

"Hello there, Pooh!" said Tigger. "I knew you were here 'cause I heard ya talkin' through the door."

"Did you see any heffalumps out there?" asked Piglet, who was poking his head around the closet door.

"Who spoke those words?" Tigger asked.

"I d-d-did," said Piglet. "Did you see any heffalumps?"

"Heffalumps!" said Tigger. "Did you check under the bed? That's the first place I always look for heffalumps."

"Yes," sighed Pooh, who had finally pulled himself out from under that very place. "We just had quite a long look under there."

"Then I guess there are no heffalumps around ta be found!" Tigger said. "What made you think there were any?"

"I'm not sure," said Pooh. "Piglet, do you remember why we were hiding from a heffalump?"

"Pooh found a box," explained Piglet.

"A box?" asked Tigger. "What's inside this box?"

"I don't know," Pooh said. "I haven't opened it."

"Allow me," said Tigger. "I happen ta be pretty good at openin' boxes."

Pooh and Piglet stood back a bit as Tigger raised the lid.

"Aha!" Tigger exclaimed. "It's a bouncin'-type thing."

"A bouncing thing?" asked Pooh.

"Look for yourself," said Tigger. Sure enough, inside the box was a strange stick bouncing around inside a circle.

"Is it a heffalump's bouncing thing?" asked Piglet.

"Hard to say," said Tigger.

"Perhaps we should ask someone," Pooh suggested.

"Good idea!" said Tigger, as he bounced right out of Piglet's house. Pooh and Piglet scrambled after him.

Soon the little trio arrived at Rabbit's garden.

"Hello, Rabbit!" cried Tigger. "Look what we found—"

"*Stop!*" cried Rabbit. "You're trampling on my turnips!"

"Don't ya wanna see our bouncin' thing?" asked Tigger.

"Oh, all right," Rabbit said and looked inside the
box. "And it just so happens that I know what this is! It's
something to be worn. See? It has straps."

"But what exactly is it, Rabbit?" asked Pooh.

"It's a . . . a . . . well, a . . . ,"
Rabbit began.

"It probably doesn't matter
anyway," came a voice from
behind them.

"Eeyore!" Tigger cried. "Glad ta see ya, buddy-boy. We're tryin' ta find out what this bouncin' thing is."

"I've already told you—it doesn't matter anyway," Eeyore said and sighed.

"Why?" asked Pooh.

"Because it's ticking. We're all doomed," Eeyore explained.

"Oh, my!" Piglet cried.

"I know exactly what it is," said Owl, who happened to be flying in to see his friend Rabbit. "I've seen it listed in one of my books—it's under X or P or maybe C. . . ."

"Hello, everyone!" came a little voice from down the path. It was Roo with Kanga and Christopher Robin.

"Keep the little guy away, Mrs. Kanga!" cried Tigger. "There's a dangerous thing over here."

"Oh, my!" Kanga exclaimed, moving back a few steps. "What kind of dangerous thing?"

"A bouncy thing with a strap in a blue box," said Pooh.

"You found it!" cried Christopher Robin.

"Found what?" asked Tigger.

"My watch!" said Christopher Robin. "I've been looking everywhere for it."

"What's a watch?" asked Pooh.

"It tells the time," answered Christopher Robin.

"Ah yes, just what I thought," Owl said wisely. "Similar to a clock, I've heard."

Christopher Robin continued to explain, "Can you hear it ticking? It ticks for every second that goes by."

"I knew it," said Eeyore, "it counts away to the end."

"The end of what?" asked Pooh.

"Don't know," said Eeyore, "just to the end."

"You strap it around your wrist," Christopher Robin said.

"I knew it!" cried Rabbit. "It's something to wear!"

Christopher Robin was feeling so grateful that he decided to celebrate. "Come on," he said. "Let's have a party. While we get everything ready, I'll tell you more about my watch."

"See these little hands?" Christopher Robin later asked. "They move around in a circle to count the hours and minutes. The fast one counts seconds."

"The bouncin' thing!" cried Tigger. "Hoo-hoo-HOO!"

"Do heffalumps wear watches?" asked Piglet.

"I suppose they could," Christopher Robin said.

"And what about the box?" asked Pooh at last. "Does that do anything?"

"That's to keep my watch safe when I'm not wearing it," Christopher Robin said.

"Ah," said Pooh, feeling quite satisfied with himself. In fact, all of the Hundred-Acre Wood friends were feeling quite satisfied now that the mystery was solved.

"Thanks for finding my watch," said Christopher Robin, "and for being such good friends."

A Place for Ariel

Ariel and her six sisters shared a bedroom in the palace. It was a large, beautiful room. But it was also a very crowded room. Ariel often felt as if she had no place for her own things and no privacy at all.

One day as Ariel sat on her bed looking at the human objects she kept in a special box, her sisters came in.

"Ariel, you missed your voice lesson again. Sebastian is very crabby with you," Attina scolded.

"And look! You've scattered your hair combs and seashells all over the room again," added Alana.

"Why don't you keep your things tidy? We all have to share this room, you know," Arista complained, as she stroked her pet sea horse.

"You're just as messy as I am," Ariel pointed out, while she collected her shells and combs.

Her sisters shook their heads. "Oh, Ariel! You're such a merbaby," said Attina.

Ariel was tired of being lectured. "I'm going to find Flounder," she snapped. "At least he isn't always fussing at me." She left in a huff, not realizing that her special box was still lying open on her bed.

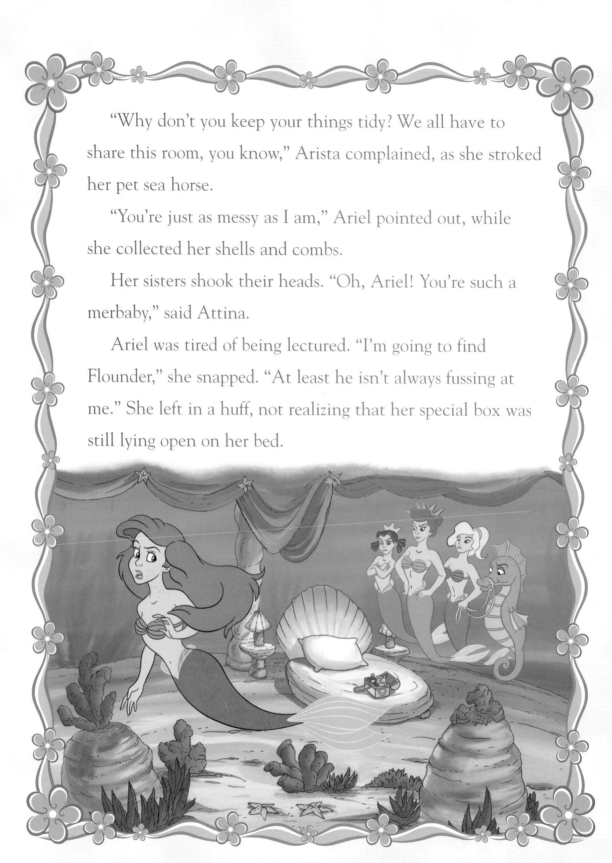

"My sisters are driving me out of my fins," Ariel complained, as she and Flounder swam along and looked for human treasures. "All I hear is 'Ariel, pick up your seashells. Ariel, put away your hair combs.' It isn't fair. I wish I had a place all of my own."

"I know what you mean, Ariel," replied Flounder. "Growing up in a school of fish doesn't exactly give me much privacy, either, you know."

Just then Ariel spotted a shining circle of metal lying on the ocean floor. "Why, Flounder, this human object reminds me of my father's crown," she said, placing it on her head.

Delighted with her new treasure, Ariel hurried back to the palace. But when she entered her bedroom, she was very surprised to see her sisters and King Triton waiting for her. Her father was holding her special box. And it was open.

"Ariel, where did you get these human objects?" Triton demanded angrily.

"Those are my treasures!" cried Ariel. "They were in my personal, private box. No one had any right to look inside it!"

"You left it out and open for anyone to see," Arista told her. "We couldn't help seeing what was in it."

"And when they saw what you were hiding, your sisters came to me at once," added Triton. "They were worried about you. And so am I. You know I don't want any human objects in my palace."

Ariel's sisters agreed.

"You're all a bunch of snoops and tattletales!" Ariel cried, grabbing her special box. "Come on, Flounder, we're leaving!"

Blinking back tears of anger, Ariel swam from the room. Flounder followed silently. For a long time, they swam farther and farther away from the palace.

Flounder began to get nervous. "Ariel, we're an awfully long way from home," he said timidly. "Don't you think we should turn back?"

Ariel was about to call Flounder a
guppy when she spotted something. "A
coral forest!" she cried. "There'll be lots of wonderful hiding
places for us! And there won't be any snoopy, sneaky big sisters
anywhere around!"

"There might be snappy, snarly big sharks around, though!"
Flounder pointed out.

But Ariel wasn't listening. She was twisting in and out
of the forest of pink and purple coral, exploring nooks and
crannies as well as finding little tunnels and hideaways.
Flounder followed her timidly. Neither of them noticed the pair
of cold yellow eyes that watched them from the shadows.

Neither of them heard the swish of a giant tail gliding closer and closer behind them.

Then all of a sudden—*snap*! Huge jaws snapped at Flounder's tail. "Ariel! Shark! Shark!" shrieked Flounder.

Ariel and Flounder swam for their lives, twisting and turning through the coral branches. But the shark was always just a few feet behind them. Suddenly Ariel saw a high wall of coral just ahead. And in the wall was a narrow crack—just big enough for them to squeeze through. Ariel pushed Flounder through the crack and squeezed in behind him. On one side of the wall was the snapping shark. Ahead of them was a long, dark tunnel.

"I d-d-don't like it here," Flounder said. "Long, dark tunnels make me dizzy."

"Well, tunnels are a whole lot better than big sharks," Ariel replied.

Just then the shark bashed its tail against the wall. The crack widened, and chunks of coral crashed down. The crack widened some more.

"Ariel, do something!" pleaded Flounder as the shark pushed its snout through the wide crack in the wall. Then it began to snap its terrible teeth at them.

Quickly Ariel grabbed the shiny metal circle from her head
and jammed it over the shark's jaws, clamping them shut.

The shark snarled and thrashed as it tried to pry the circle
from its jaws. The shark's tail hit the wall again. This time,
the coral crumbled completely. Falling chunks knocked Ariel
and Flounder away.

With a fearful cry, they darted into the tunnel. Twisting
and turning, Ariel and Flounder reached the end. They were
in a tiny cave, called a grotto! The floor was soft and sandy.
Above them, light streamed down through the broken wall.

Many little nooks, crannies, and tiny shelves had formed in the walls of the soft, pastel coral that surrounded them.

Unable to enter the grotto, the shark snarled and swam away.

"Say good-bye to old greedy jaws!" Flounder said, with a sigh of relief.

"I think that shark helped me, Flounder," replied Ariel.

"He did?" a surprised Flounder asked.

"Yes. We would never have found this grotto if he hadn't chased us," Ariel explained. "And just look! It's a perfect place of my own. Why, I can keep my human treasures here and not worry about making Daddy angry."

Humming happily, Ariel arranged her human objects around the grotto. Then she and Flounder headed back to the palace.

Ariel was so happy that she didn't even mind when she saw her father and sisters waiting for her. Ariel's sisters rushed to greet her. "We were worried about you," Attina said. "We're all very sorry that we snooped, but guess what? Daddy has decided we need more space, so he's going to build each of us a new bedroom!"

"That's right, Ariel," said King Triton, smiling at his youngest daughter. "After all, every daughter needs a special place of her very own!"

"Or even two special places," Ariel whispered to Flounder, with a wink. Then with her head full of happy plans for her two special places, Ariel gave her father the biggest hug he had had all day.

The Lost Boys were bored. They had already played Follow the Leader with Michael and John. They had played Pirates and Pan with their pretend swords. And they had stomped through swamps and swung through trees. But now they were so bored that they were beginning to fall asleep.

"There's nothing to do," Slightly yawned.

"We need a new game," said Tootles.

John thought for a minute. "I know! Let's have a treasure hunt!"

That woke up Slightly—and all the other Lost Boys.

Jumping up and down, Little Michael agreed, "Yes, John!"

The Lost Boys crowded around John and Michael. They were so excited that none of them saw Mr. Smee sneaking up through the trees behind them.

"I'll make a map for the treasure," said John.

The Lost Boys cheered. This sounded like fun! John took a piece of paper and a pencil and went off into the woods. The Lost Boys started to follow him.

But Michael stopped them. "No peeking!" he said.

The Lost Boys grumbled a little, but they sat down to wait for John to come back.

Meanwhile, Mr. Smee hurried back to Captain Hook's ship. "A treasure—a treasure!" Mr. Smee cried gleefully. "Oh, Captain Hook will be happy to hear about this! Ho, ho—yes, he will!"

Captain Hook was indeed happy to hear about the treasure. "Any treasure in Never Land is *mine*, Smee," said Hook. "We'll get that map and that treasure!"

Excited, Smee danced a sailor's jig. But Hook conked him on the head.

"Get back to the rowing boat. We're going ashore," Hook ordered.

Slowly, John wandered through the forest. First he had to think of some kind of treasure for the Lost Boys to find. That was the hardest part. Once he found that, drawing the map would be easy.

After a while, John sat down on a log to think. "Treasure," he said aloud, "silver, rubies, and gold." A bee buzzed past his head. John started to wave it away, but the bee wasn't interested in him. As John watched, the bee headed straight for the hollow of a tree. "Gold," John said again and smiled.

Standing on his tiptoes, John could just see inside the tree. And what his eyes couldn't see, his ears and nose told him. There were bees buzzing inside the tree. There was a sweet smell coming from inside the tree. There had to be a honeycomb inside—a honeycomb with golden honey in it!

"That's a pretty good treasure," decided John. He and the Lost Boys had found honey before, so they would know how to get the honeycomb without getting stung.

John walked back through the woods. He drew his
map as he went and then added a clue: *Take the treasure
carefully—its guards are as fierce as they can be.*

John laughed and thought, "They'll have fun working
this out."

Suddenly a hand clamped over his mouth. Mr. Smee
pulled John behind a tree.

"We'll take that!" demanded Captain Hook as he grabbed the treasure map. "So kind of you to do all the work," he said mockingly.

John struggled, but soon Mr. Smee had him tied to the tree with a rag around his mouth. "Don't worry," he said, patting John on the shoulder. "The Lost Boys will know how to find another lost boy."

Hook and Smee gleefully set off after the treasure.

The Lost Boys were still bored. "Shouldn't John be back by now?" asked Tootles.

"Yeah, how long does it take to make a treasure map?" asked Slightly.

And so, the Lost Boys set out towards the woods.

"No peeking," Michael reminded them. Slightly stopped and looked at the Lost Boys. "Well, we can't peek if we don't know what we're looking for, can we?" he asked.

Michael agreed that Slightly was right, and he wanted to go with the Lost Boys. "All right," Michael said.

The Lost Boys cheered and ran into the woods. The first thing they found was John.

Slightly untied the rag around John's mouth.

"Hook took the treasure map!" John exclaimed.

"He'll find the treasure—*our* treasure!" cried Tootles, and he stamped his foot.

The Lost Boys were ready to run off, but John stopped them. "Wait," he said. "I have an idea."

John led the Lost Boys close to the honey tree. They could hear Mr. Smee and Hook trying to work out the last clue on the treasure map.

"Oh no!" shouted John. "Hook has found the treasure tree!" he said, pointing at the honey tree.

"You're too late!" Hook said, as he smiled his nastiest smile. He boosted Smee up to the hole in the tree.

Mr. Smee reached in—and got a handful of honey. "Oh, sticky, sticky, sticky!" Smee cried, as he tried to shake the honey off his hand.

The honey splattered all over Hook's coat. Then the tree began to buzz.

All of a sudden the bees came pouring out of the tree.

They chased Hook and Smee all the way back to their rowing boat.

Once the pirates were out of sight, the boys cheered.

Slightly picked up the treasure map that Hook had dropped. "*Take the treasure carefully—its guards are as fierce as they can be,*" he read. Slightly looked over at the tree and added, "I think those guards have gone."

"But the treasure's still there!" Michael clapped excitedly.

John carefully took the golden honeycomb out of the tree. The Lost Boys carried it back to their hideout and made a sticky-sweet mess.

Some time later, the bees buzzed back to their tree and began making more honey.

Meanwhile, on board a certain pirate ship, a bee-stung Captain Hook drank a cup of tea—without honey!

Early one morning many, many years from now . . .

"Waaak!" squawked Donald Duck when his fully automatic, quicker-getter-upper bed flipped over and dumped him on the floor. "I'll never get used to that bed," he muttered, staggering towards the bathroom.

His new Bathroom of the 22nd Century had been installed just yesterday. Daisy Duck had insisted he have the most modern bathroom. The company that created the Bathroom of the 22nd Century was the biggest account at Daisy's advertising agency. Her award-winning slogan of "Fresh as a Daisy" had made Daisy a trillionaire.

Donald sighed, entered the bathroom, and pressed the start button. "Good morning, Mr. Duck," said a computer voice. The bathroom whirled into action. Robot arms removed Donald's pyjamas and squeezed toothpaste onto his toothbrush. Another pair of arms brushed his teeth and then placed him in the wash-and-fluff-o-rama shower.

"Ah," sighed Donald. Not-too-hot, not-too-cold water doused him from all sides. "This is wonderful!" he moaned, as the automated shower washed, shampooed, fluff-dried, and put his bathrobe on him—all in two minutes flat.

But the one innovation that Donald wouldn't let Daisy install was the Automatic Dresser of the 22nd Century. He had his own special style of dressing.

Donald left the house and hailed a passing helicopter-taxi. He was meeting Daisy for breakfast at Clarabelle's Café.

"Good morning, Donald dear," Daisy called. "How's your Bathroom of the 22nd Century?"

"Fresh as a Daisy!" said Donald.

Daisy laughed and ordered her breakfast.

Clarabelle gave the order to her electronic hands-free order pad. "That's one Daisy Duck special—a wheat-grass-vitamin-super-organic-power shake."

Ten minutes later, Donald dropped Daisy off at her office. Then he took the heli-cab to his ship, the *Miss Daisy 2001*.

"Good morning, Captain," said a computer voice when Donald stepped on board. As the *Miss Daisy* headed out to sea, the automatic fishing rods saluted their captain; then each baited its own hook, cast out the line, and reeled in a fish. Soon the fishing rods started tossing fish into the tank. Donald paced the deck, looking for something to do.

"Fishing used to be an adventure," thought Donald, sighing. "This is kind of boring," he said.

Suddenly a bottle fished from the sea whacked him on the head. "*Waaaak!*" Donald cried. "What a strange-looking bottle," muttered Donald.

"I wonder what's inside. Maybe it's a genie who will grant me three wishes!"

Donald opened the bottle, and a large cloud of smoke drifted skyward. Lights flashed—but no genie. Then the smoke cleared and a computer screen appeared.

"This is the genie," a recorded voice mail said. "I'm sorry that I'm not in to grant your wishes. Due to the high volume of bottle-wishing, only one wish can be granted at this time. Please select from the following options: press button 1 for romance, 2 for adventure, and 3 for—"

"Adventure! Oh, boy!" exclaimed Donald, quickly pressing button 2. In the blink of an eye, Donald found himself in front of an old-fashioned log cabin next to a lake.

Donald spotted a fishing rod and jumped into a canoe. "It's been a long time since I paddled a can—*Oof! Waaak!*" cried Donald as he fell into the lake. "*Brr!*" he shivered, struggling to get back into the canoe.

Donald dropped the fishing line into the water. In just a few minutes, he felt a tug. "A bite!" he cried. Soon Donald had landed the fish and paddled back to shore. "Ah, this is the life!" exclaimed Donald.

Inside the cabin, Donald saw a small pile of wood next to an old wood-burning stove. "Hmmm, I think I need some more wood," he said to himself.

So Donald loaded himself up with firewood that he found behind the cabin. But as Donald staggered towards the door, he tripped. The wood went flying and some logs hit him on the head. "*Yeow!*" he cried.

Donald stumbled into the cabin and loaded all the wood into the stove. Then he found some strips of cloth to wrap around his bruised head. He took off his wet sailor suit and hung it over the stove.

Donald was cleaning the fish when he smelled smoke. "Yikes—my sailor suit!" he cried. He grabbed his suit just before it caught fire.

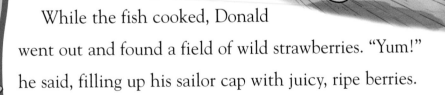

While the fish cooked, Donald went out and found a field of wild strawberries. "Yum!" he said, filling up his sailor cap with juicy, ripe berries.

Unfortunately, a family of bears was also picking berries. One look from mama bear sent Donald racing back to the cabin, right through a patch of thorny bushes. "*Ouch! Ow! Yeow!*" he cried.

All in all, it hadn't been the best morning of Donald's life. But none of his misadventures could keep Donald from cooking the most delicious dish—fish à la strawberries. He was just about to take a bite, when Donald found himself back on the *Miss Daisy 2001*! His fish à la strawberries had completely disappeared, and he was left holding the bottle. The tank was full of fish, and his ship was heading slowly back to the dock.

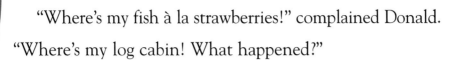

"Where's my fish à la strawberries!" complained Donald. "Where's my log cabin! What happened?"

Another large cloud of smoke from the bottle drifted upwards and lights flashed—but again, no genie. The genie's voice mail said, "We're sorry. Your wish has been deleted due to a computer malfunction. Unfortunately, terminated wishes can't be granted again. We're sorry for any inconvenience this may have caused. Please return the bottle to the sea so that we may serve others."

Donald threw the bottle overboard and stomped off the ship.

"Donald!" cried Daisy when she met him that evening at Clarabelle's Café. "What happened? Your head is bandaged! Your face is scratched! Your suit is burned, and your cap is stained red!"

Donald explained all about the bottle, the wish, the canoe, the log cabin, the wood-burning stove, the wild strawberries, the thorny bushes, and the bears—and what a great time he had had!

"You mean it was fun to fall in a lake, drop wood on your head, burn your clothes, run through some thorny bushes, get chased by bears, and cook your own food?" Daisy asked.

"Well," began Donald, "a few of the parts were more fun than others."

"Would you pay money to do it all over again?" Daisy asked, smiling.

"Sure," Donald said. "But the chances of finding that genie's bottle again—"

"What should I call it?" Daisy interrupted. Her eyes twinkled with the spark of an idea.

"Call what?" asked Donald.

"The theme park," she replied.

"What theme park?" Donald asked.

"An adventure theme park," Daisy explained. "Where visitors do all the things that 22nd-century machines do now. I'll have a lake for fishing, canoes, fields of wild berries, and log cabins with wood-burning stoves. I could even put mechanical bears in the berry fields."

When Clarabelle came over to take their orders, Daisy stood up. "Where are you going?" Donald asked.

"Back to the office," said Daisy. "This idea is fabulous. I'll get started right away!"

Donald sighed. Then he looked at Clarabelle. "I'll have the fish à la strawberries, please."

Thunderbolt raced across the TV screen with Dirty Dawson just behind him. "I'll get you, you varmint!" Dawson snarled, swinging a heavy net as if it were a lasso.

"Run, Thunderbolt!" called Lucky, as he watched in the living room of the Dalmatian Plantation. "You can beat the lily-liver, goose-gizzard Dirty Dawson rotter!"

"Why, Lucky! What kind of language is that?" Perdita shut off the TV.

"Dirty Dawson always talks like that," Lucky said to his mother.

"Then I think it's time for you to stop listening to Dirty Dawson," Perdita told him. "I want you to go outside and play. That's much better than watching TV."

"But—"

"Now, Lucky," Perdita said firmly.

Lucky walked slowly outside. It was so boring out there. There was never anything to do. He lay down, feeling sorry for himself, and put his chin on his paws. But suddenly he brightened up as he spotted a big brown box waiting for the rubbish man. Its front was cut out, and to Lucky, it looked just like a TV! Patch was napping inside; but other than that, the box was perfect. "If I can't watch TV," Lucky thought, "maybe I can *play* it!"

"Wake up, Patch!" Lucky said. "We're going to put on the Thunderbolt show right here."

"Huh?" said a sleepy Patch.

"Let's see," Lucky continued, "Rolly can do the Kanine Krunchies commercial, and Penny can be the announcer."

Patch was wide awake now. "Who do I get to be?"

"Dirty Dawson," Lucky replied.

Patch wrinkled his nose. "Why do I have to be the bad guy?" he asked.

"Because you already have the black eye," explained Lucky.

Rolly and Penny wandered over, and Lucky told them what their roles would be. "And soon," he added, as he left to find a costume for himself, "Thunderbolt will be here!" Because the show was his idea, Lucky decided that he would play Thunderbolt.

"Thunderbolt!" Rolly and Penny exclaimed, wagging their tails. "Here? That's what he said, isn't it, Patch?"

"He said that they're going to put on the Thunderbolt show right here!" Patch nodded and said. "We should practice our—"

"We should go and tell everyone!" Rolly and Penny said and ran off to tell the beagle family, who lived across the field. Then Penny raced off to tell the dachshunds, who lived down the road. Patch hurried to tell all his other sisters and brothers. Soon all the puppies were telling their friends. By the time Lucky came back to the box with a magazine photo he meant to use as a Thunderbolt mask, the backyard was filled with hundreds of pups and dogs, yapping excitedly.

They became even more excited when Lucky stepped up to the box to announce the show.

It took a minute before Lucky could make out their words.

"Thunderbolt's coming!"

"A real star in our own backyard!"

"Lucky's so clever to invite him!"

"Do you think he'll bring Kanine Krunchies?" asked Rolly.

Then the dogs began flooding Lucky with questions. "When will he be here, Lucky? Where's Thunderbolt?"

"Wait a minute," Lucky said weakly, and he ducked behind the box and dropped the picture he was carrying. What was he going to do? He couldn't go out there in disguise now. Everyone would know it wasn't the real Thunderbolt. The yapping and barking were becoming so loud that Lucky couldn't even think of a plan.

Suddenly a commanding bark rose above the noise. Lucky peeked around the box just in time to see a sleek chauffeured limousine stop in front of their house. Leaning out of the back window was the real Thunderbolt!

"Hello, youngsters!" barked Thunderbolt. As the chauffeur got out of the car, Thunderbolt let himself out through the

window. The mob of puppies and dogs raced over to him. Lucky slipped out from behind the box, but he hung back when he saw his parents coming out of the house. He would be in trouble now!

Then Lucky heard his father say, "Well, hello, Thunderbolt. This is quite a surprise." Pongo looked around at the puppies and dogs. "Yet your fan club certainly seems to be here."

Thunderbolt nodded and said, "It's a surprise for me, too. My pet and I were returning from the location where we were shooting an episode. I'm afraid my pet lost his way. When we saw the crowd here, I knew we would find help."

"Oh yes, our pets will help," Perdita said happily. "They're very kind."

Thunderbolt smiled as Roger and Anita came out of the house to talk to the chauffeur. "Actually, when I saw all the Dalmatians," Thunderbolt explained, "I realized this must be the home of the famous Pongos. All of dogdom knows you. We were so pleased when you recovered the pups. I was about to set out on a search myself when I heard that you had found them."

"How thoughtful," said Perdita.

Just then Lucky found the courage to talk to Thunderbolt. After all, he had promised the others a Thunderbolt show. "Would you show us some of your tricks, Thunderbolt?" Lucky asked.

Perdita smiled and said, "This is my son Lucky. He's your biggest fan." Then she nudged Lucky playfully. "But the way he sometimes talks, I think he's a Dirty Dawson fan, too."

Thunderbolt bowed. "I would be delighted to perform for the Pongos." He turned to Lucky and said, "All right, son, you can be Dirty Dawson. But don't speak the way he does. No dog wants to sound like that."

Lucky nodded seriously, and Perdita smiled.

"Ready?" Thunderbolt called to Lucky. Then in a flash, Thunderbolt streaked across the backyard with Lucky close behind. Without warning, Thunderbolt stopped in his tracks, turned, and soared through the air right over Lucky's head.

"That's my fast getaway," Thunderbolt told them.

The puppies and dogs barked their approval as
Thunderbolt raced around in circles. Then all of a sudden
he disappeared. The puppies and dogs looked around,
astonished. Just as suddenly Thunderbolt leapt from
behind a couple of boxes, surprising them all. "When a
boulder isn't handy," he said, "I take any hiding place I
can find. The trick is to be so quick that Dirty Dawson
can't tell where I've gone."

Thunderbolt's pet came out of the house with the Dalmatians' pets. "I'm afraid I must go," said Thunderbolt. "It was a pleasure meeting you youngsters and a privilege to meet your brave parents. The next time we're here on location, you must come to see me."

But before Thunderbolt left, he posed for pictures that Roger and Anita took. "This gives me an idea for a song, Anita," Roger said.

Pongo, Perdita, all the Dalmatian puppies, and their friends barked and yapped their thanks to Thunderbolt.

Perdita watched Thunderbolt climb into the car, and then
he leaned out the window to give one final farewell bark.

"He's quite a gentledog, isn't he, dear?" Perdita said to Pongo.

"Yes, he is," said Pongo, nodding heartily.

"Perhaps it isn't so bad for the children to watch his show,"
she added.

"I think you're right, Perdy," Pongo agreed.

The puppies barked their agreement, too.

Lucky was still watching the car drive off. "You know,
Mother, you were right about other things, too. I shouldn't talk

like Dirty Dawson," said Lucky. Then he grinned and added, "And playing outside was much better than watching TV!"

Perdita nodded and said, "Yes, dear. I think we all learned something today."

"I learned that Lucky puts on the best shows ever," said Patch. "What will you do next, Lucky?" he asked, as Lucky went over to the box.

But Lucky was already fast asleep, dreaming about his next adventure with Thunderbolt.

Alice and the Giant Dormouse

Alice sat at the tea party with the Mad Hatter
and the March Hare, wishing someone would offer her
something to eat and drink. It wasn't polite to help
herself, but she was *so* thirsty. "I'll just pour myself a
small cup of tea," she said quietly.

But as Alice began to pour the tea, a sleepy little
Dormouse popped out of the teapot.

"*Eeek!*" shrieked Alice, who wasn't used to dormice—or any sort of mice—popping out of teapots. She dropped the teapot and watched it roll down the table, twirling the Dormouse until he was pink in the face.

As Alice lunged to catch the teapot, a small box fell from her apron pocket. On the outside were the words *Eat me* and inside the box were magical candies.

It was the box she had found when she first fell into Wonderland! She had tucked it into her pocket before she shrank and fell into the pool of tears. But before she could put the box back into her pocket, the Mad Hatter grabbed it.

"What's this? 'Eat me!' Eat what?" asked the Mad Hatter. He opened the box and found the tiny candies. "Why, these look delicious," he said.

Just as the Mad Hatter started to pop one into his mouth, Alice cried, "No! Don't eat it!" She knocked it from the Mad Hatter's hand, and it flew into the air and landed in the Dormouse's teapot.

For a moment nothing happened. Then the teapot began to rumble and shake. It cracked into many pieces and out of it rose the Dormouse, growing bigger and bigger by the second.

"*Eeeeek!*" screamed the Mad Hatter and the March Hare. They ducked under the table, which was sagging under the Dormouse's increasing weight.

"*Aaah!*" cried the Dormouse as he stretched, and the table broke in half.

"Help!" squealed the Mad Hatter and the March Hare.

But the Dormouse just blinked and stumbled sleepily away, leaving footprints the size of fishponds in the Mad Hatter's flower beds. Rubbing his eyes, the Dormouse crashed through the garden gate and wandered down the path.

As he stumbled along, Alice could hear branches crashing and the birds shrieking while they watched his head go past their nests.

"I must stop the Dormouse before he smashes Wonderland to bits!" exclaimed Alice. She ran after him, but with his huge legs, the Dormouse was soon out of sight.

"Looking for someone?" a voice said from above Alice's head. She looked up and saw the Cheshire Cat grinning at her from a branch.

"Do you know which way the giant Dormouse went?" asked Alice.

"Follow his trail," the Cheshire Cat answered. He pointed to a spot by the path where the bushes were as flat as pancakes. "He's taking little naps along the way."

"Thank you," replied Alice, and she ran on. She passed squashed shrubs, broken bushes, flattened flowers, and mashed mushrooms; but she still didn't find the Dormouse.

At last, Alice came to the Caterpillar, who sat smoking his pipe. "O, U again," said the Caterpillar when he saw her. "Y R U still here?" he puffed.

"Have you seen a very large Dormouse come this way?" Alice asked.

"S Ndeed," the Caterpillar slowly replied. "E mashed the mushrooms. Find M N make M small again."

"U R right—er, you are right," said Alice. "That's what I want to do, but I'm not sure how."

"Take some of that mushroom with U," the Caterpillar suggested. "I would tell U which side makes U small, but I can't recall which is which."

"I'll just take a bit of both," decided Alice, breaking two chunks from the mushroom.

Suddenly she heard shrieks coming from the flower garden. When Alice raced into the garden, she found the Dormouse napping with his toes in the flowers.

"A monster is sleeping in our beds!" the flowers yelled. "He's bending our stems and pulling our petals!"

Alice knew that if she fed the Dormouse the shrinking piece of mushroom, he would get small again. But if she fed him the growing bit by mistake, he would get even bigger.

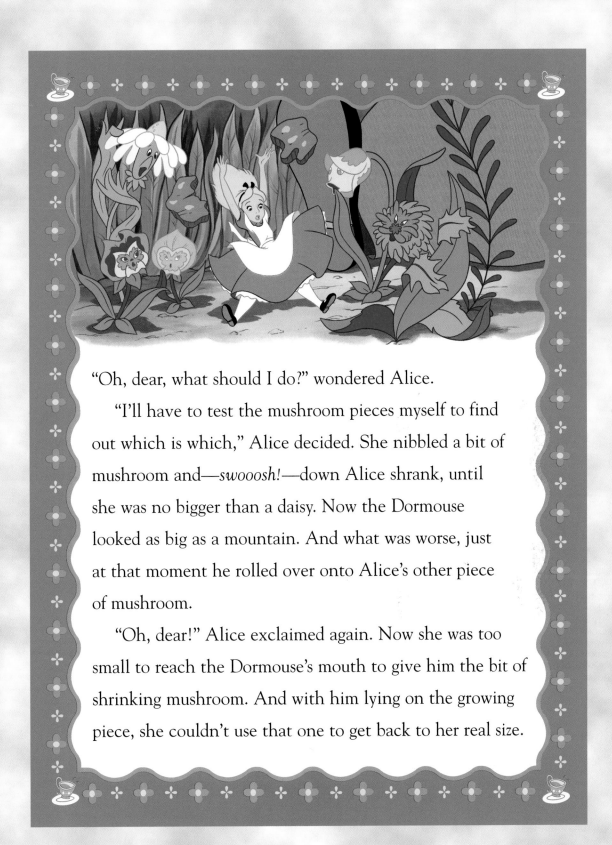

"Oh, dear, what should I do?" wondered Alice.

"I'll have to test the mushroom pieces myself to find out which is which," Alice decided. She nibbled a bit of mushroom and—*swoooosh!*—down Alice shrank, until she was no bigger than a daisy. Now the Dormouse looked as big as a mountain. And what was worse, just at that moment he rolled over onto Alice's other piece of mushroom.

"Oh, dear!" Alice exclaimed again. Now she was too small to reach the Dormouse's mouth to give him the bit of shrinking mushroom. And with him lying on the growing piece, she couldn't use that one to get back to her real size.

Alice thought and thought, "Somehow I have to wake him up. Then I could ask him to move, to nibble the shrinking piece of mushroom, or to . . . to . . . Oh, dear, I have to do something!" she wailed.

So Alice shouted at the Dormouse. She tugged at his fur. She even tickled his paws. But nothing woke him.

"Whistle loudly in his ear!" yelled the trumpet vines.

"Bite him on the knee!" growled a tiger lily.

"Stick him with thorns," the roses suggested.

Suddenly the Cheshire Cat appeared in the pansy bed. "Whisper the word *cat* in his ear, my dear," he told Alice, just before he faded away.

"But how am I supposed to reach his ear?" Alice cried. "It's way up there, and I'm way down here!"

Just then a rocking-horse fly fluttered by. Alice jumped on its back. Clutching the bit of shrinking mushroom in her hand, she flew up to the Dormouse's ear.

"Cat!" she whispered. "Cat, kitty, kitty, pussycat!"

"Caaaaaaaatt!" shrieked the Dormouse.

Quickly Alice threw the bit of mushroom into the Dormouse's open mouth.

Swoosh! Instantly the Dormouse shrank to his normal size. Alice landed with a thump and scooped up the bit of mushroom that would make her grow. It was mashed because the Dormouse had been lying on it, but she didn't care. She nibbled and—*swoosh!*— Alice was her own size again.

The Dormouse was still running in circles, yelling about cats. Gently, Alice picked him up and popped him into her pocket.

By the time she arrived back at the Mad Hatter's house, the Dormouse was dozing again. As the Mad Hatter and March Hare watched nervously, Alice tucked the dreaming Dormouse into a new teapot and put the lid on.

"He's himself again," Alice assured them. "But you really should watch what he eats."

And with that, Alice went off to find the White Rabbit. Maybe he would know how she could get home.